The Zanzibar Zoo

Jewel Prediletto

Jewel Prediletto

Illustrated by Delores Messenger

This book belongs to:

Dedicated to:
ALL THE CHILDREN OF THE WORLD
WHO
LOVE
TO
GO
TO
THE
ZOO

Published by
Hara Publishing
P.O. Box 19732
Seattle, WA 98109
(425) 775-7868

ISBN: 1-883697-93-X
Library of Congress Number: 2002105616

Printed in Canada

Zoe and her brother Zandar love to go to the Zanzibar Zoo!

There they see Zenobia the Zebra and Zinnia, her little one, too.

Now Zippy and Zita prefer Zulu the Zebu and her little Ziggy, who live there too.

Does it sound like fun at the Zanzibar Zoo?

Now Zeke and Zoella like everything there.

Be it Zebra or Zebu, they don't care.

They like to see Zak the Yak and his momma Zella.

They also like Penny the Panda, and her little Ella.

But Zoe and her brother Zandar go to the Zanzibar Zoo,

Mostly to see Zenobia the Zebra and Zinnia, her little one, too!

Zane, **Zed**, and **Zee**

know how to climb a tree.

Zoe and **Zandar** think it's silly to.

Zippy and **Zita** think it's fun,

but they'd rather run.

What would **you** want to do?

Zeke and **Z**oella are plenty good fellas.

They say: "Whatever we play is up to you."

Zesty and **Z**ealous are never jealous

of other people's plans, so they say:

"Whatever you choose, we just can't lose.

It's all good fun, it's all good play."

They climbed a tree, they ran after a ball,

they took, to a sick friend, a little doll.

Then they
all walked to the
Zanzibar Zoo.

Well now,
they've all learned
a lesson today,
it's true!

and everyone
out there, have **you?**

The **Zoo,** the **Zoo,** the **Zanzibar Zoo**, my favorite of any park.

The first thing I'll go to see is **Arvid,** the Ant-eating **Aardvark.**

And you, have you ever seen **Armand,** the **Armadillo**

at a Zoological park?

And **Barona** the **Bear** and her cubs three

are

happily climbing

another

tree.

Bo the **Baboon** calls with a very loud bark

to my friends and to me.

He wants attention for himself and his fellow

Baboons in the tree.

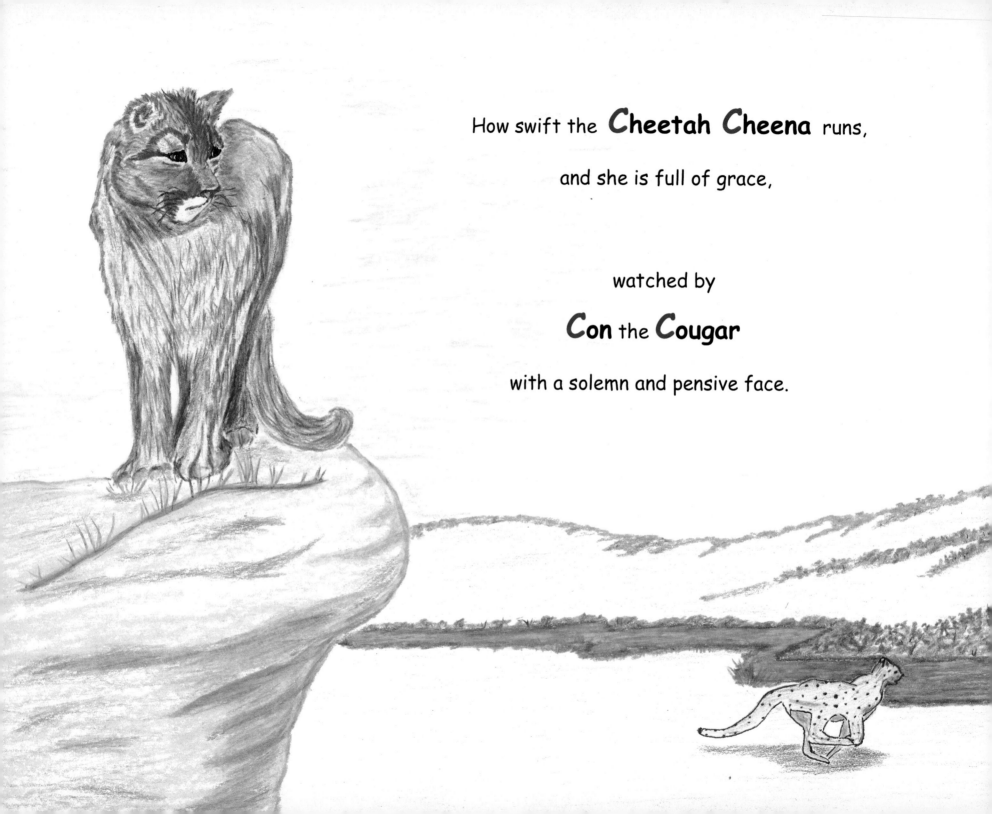

How swift the **Cheetah Cheena** runs,

and she is full of grace,

watched by

Con the **Cougar**

with a solemn and pensive face.

Deedee the **Deer**

is endearing and loved

by each of the workers there,

and just as much loved by visitors

from **everywhere!**

Ooo... look at **Devi** the **Dingo,**

an **Aussie** is he,

who runs to the fence

and wants to be free.

Emma the Emu
and Emeer her mate,

march around in a silly state

With Effie and Eddie

matching their gait,

calling their parents to wait

Elmo the Elephant is the biggest you'll see,

in any Zoo anywhere.

Everyone loves him in Zanzibar,

so be sure to visit him there.

Ferrel the **F**erret and
Freddie the **F**ox are side by side
at the **Z**oo.
They come to the fence
to peer at the folks,
since they want
attention too!

Girra the **Giraffe** and **Girro,** her son,

a stiff-legged, long necked pair,

so silly to see and of gawkers

too, get their share.

What a pretty **Gazelle Gaziba** is,

and **Gaily,** her baby, is too.

Be sure to see them at

the **Zanzibar Zoo!**

Hena Hyena and **Hershal,**

the baby of hers,

hide in their den behind

foliage and burrs.

While **Hilda** the **Horse** whinnies and neighs,

and her little **Harry**

frolicks and plays.

Iggy Iguana is surely a sight.

He's friendly enough so don't have a fright.

and **Ivan** the **Ibex** is some sort of king,

perched high on his rock where he is seen.

Jack rabbit **J**ay, long-eared and long-legged,

he hops and he hides,

because **J**ake the **J**ackal looks hungrily on him from where he abides.

Kangaroo Jane and her little **Joey**

are surely a sassy sight to behold.

They feel safe and secure here at the Zoo,

so are very friendly and bold.

And who wouldn't want to cuddle **Kay** the **Koala**

and her soft little **Kandy?**

We'll buy a toy mamma and baby to take home

so we'll always have them handy.

Lima the **Llama** is pretty and trim,

and so is her son by the name of **Jim.**

They aren't real crazy about **Leo the Lion**

and **Lily** his lady.

They don't even like **Larry and Lena,**

their cute little babies.

Mack the **Maki**

is quite alone.

His ringed tail is useful and long.

His

neighbor

beside him

is **Macy** the

Macaw, with

colorful feathers

but a very

loud **caw.**

Nero

the **Newt**

is not very cute,

but he is a

resident

there.

As is **Nita** the **Nightingale** and her charming pair.

Orin

the **O**wl

is a bird of the night.

He gives the mice

a **terrible fright!**

Peri the **O**pposum,

her family on back,

is **funny** to see!

Probably thinks the **same thing** of me.

But stranger than any you'll no doubt agree,

is **Patsy Platypus,** a funny form,

who'll you'll laugh to see.

With duck-like bill,

and lays eggs, and is furry,

and dives into the pool in a **real** hurry.

And who doesn't love **Penny** the **Panda**

and baby **Ella,** too,

who live their lives munching bamboo?

There's **Quinton** the **Quail**. The only "**Q**"

who is residing at the **Zoo**.

Black rings around his shiny eyes,

focused on his feed,

Racy Racoon is washing it off

and pays me no heed.

The **Rhinocerous** whom they call **Rhino**

cannot see very well,

but he makes up for it

with his excellent hearing,

and sense of smell!

Sassy the **Sasin,**

his horns are curly and long,

you see.

He is from **India.**

Do you suppose that is where

he'd rather be?

The pretty **Sable,** whose name is **Mable,**

is better off at the **Zoo,** I think,

than as part of a coat,

whose cost would make you **blink!**

Look at **Tess** the **T**angum
as she lovingly looks at her foal **T**ango.

They're a pair of ponies from **T**ibet,

You mean you didn't know?

You'll nearly never see

Tappi the **T**apir with his flexible snout.

Because, unless it's night time,

Tapirs don't usually come out.

The **Umbrella Bird**
who they call **Umber,**

is a different sight to see.

And you must look high up

to catch a glimpse of him

in his lofty tree.

They share a native place

along the **Amazon**

with the **U**akari.

And here they do too--

a **double rarity!**

See **Victoria** the **Vicuna**
and her little **Vanessa**.
We are happy they are here at the **Zoo**.
They are from **South America**
along with the **Viscacha**
who lives here too!

Another **Aussie** is

Whoopsie the **Wombat**,

a rotund little marsupial is she.

She has her baby in a pouch,

and he's **impossible** to see.

Let's look at **Wanda**

the **Wapiti**

and little one, called **Willi.**

Her mate, **Walli,**

is the biggest

Elk

you'll

ever

see!

Xenicidae? Here's a pair that's very rare,

Xaviar and **Xandi.**

We're happy to see them with their babies,

Curtis and **Candi.**

Zak the **Y**ak and his momma **Z**ella

graze on grass and gaze at us too.

We enjoy this pair at the **Z**anzibar **Z**oo.

And of course we cannot forget **Zenobia** the **Zebra** and **Zenia,** her little one,

who **Zoe** and **Zandar** find very much fun!

Zippy and **Zita** are happy, too,

that **Ziggy** and **Zulu,**

the **Zebus,**

are here

at the

Zoo.

There is much more,

and I'm sure you'll agree,

that the **Zanzibar Zoo**

has animals from

A

to

Z!